Ginny

Debbie

Love
Diane

The Little Girl Who Did . . . WHAT?!!!

Story by Diane Dupuy

Illustrated by Ed Stockelbach

The Little Girl Who Did...WHAT?!!! is a trademark of Beyond Blacklight Inc.

Canadian Cataloguing in Publication Data

Dupuy, Diane
The Little Girl Who Did...WHAT?!!!

ISBN 0-9730736-0-8

I. Children's books   II. Dupuy, Diane   III. Title
IV. Dare To Dream   V. Throw Your Heart Over the Fence

Printed in Canada by Friesens

Illustrations by **Ed Stockelbach**
It takes special people to work with special people and Ed Stockelbach is more special than he realizes. Always giving. Always caring. Always loving...and forever being the little boy who farts butterflies.

Editing/Book Project Coordinating by **Fina Scroppo**
Her guidance was so powerful that she has created a child through this endeavour. A diamond in the rough, she sparkled with enthusiasm and patience throughout the labour of giving birth to this story.

Special thanks to **Matie Molinaro** – literary agent extraordinaire!
Special thanks to **Famous PEOPLE Players staff** for their patience, encouragement and support.

If you can't find **The Little Girl Who Did...WHAT?!!!** where you shop, ask your retailer to give us a call. Meanwhile, we offer a mail-order service for your convenience and an aggressive discount schedule for orders of more than 10 books. Please call us to find out the details.

Beyond Blacklight Inc.
33 Lisgar St.
Toronto, ON M6J 3T3

(416) 532-1137; fax: (416) 532-1169
Toll-free: 1-888-453-3385
Website: www.fpp.org
E-mail: fpp@globalserve.net

A great gift for every occasion, for birthdays, graduations, Mother's Day, Father's Day or any day.

Coming soon...**The Little Girl Who Lost Her Tickles.**

To my daughters…Joanne, who came into the world farting butterflies and to her sister, Jeannine, who flies after them.

With love forever,

Mother

ONCE UPON A TIME, there was
a very narrow village, sandwiched between
two tall, dark, very narrow mountains.
Everyone who lived in the narrow village
felt so safe living between the two tall,
narrow mountains that they became very
narrow-minded.

The streets were very narrow, the houses
were narrow, and all the schools and shops
were narrow. The people were narrow, and
the food they ate was narrow. Even the little
mice, who lived in their narrow houses, ate
narrow cheese.

Why, even the hospital where all the children were born was narrow.

Every morning, the narrow nurse would line up the new babies in a narrow row for everyone to admire.

All the babies looked the same, tucked in their narrow cribs in their narrow room, waiting to be taken home by their narrow parents.

The nurse stopped to check on the newest baby who had just arrived…a little girl.

Everything about this little girl, in her
narrow crib, looked normal…that
was until the nurse picked her up to
give her a hug and…

OOPS!
The little girl
farted a butterfly!

The narrow nurse went running to the narrow doctor for help! She whispered in the doctor's narrow ear to tell him what had happened.

The narrow doctor was so horrified that he screamed,
"She did what?!!!"

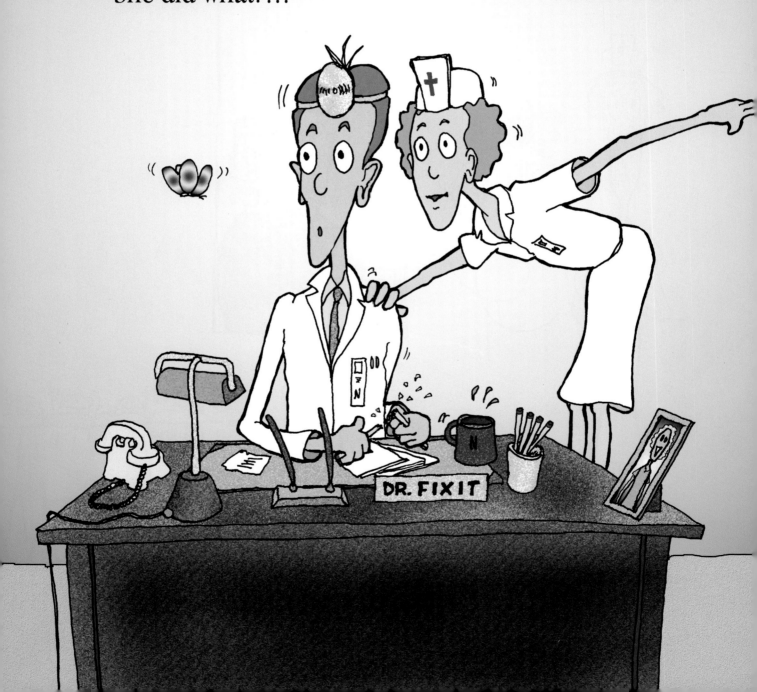

The narrow doctor and the narrow nurse went running to catch the butterfly, but now there wasn't just one butterfly to catch…

but 100 butterflies!

The little girl couldn't stop herself! She kept on farting butterflies!

The narrow doctor, who looked like a narrow weasel, went to tell the little girl's narrow parents the shocking news!

When the narrow parents heard what had happened, they screamed,
"She did what?!!!"

"What can we do?"

The narrow doctor scratched his head. He had never met anyone like this little girl. There is no cure!

"She is different," said the narrow doctor. "She will never be like the other narrow children because...your little girl farts butterflies."

Sadly, the narrow parents took the
little girl home from the narrow
hospital to live on their very narrow street.

Putting her in her narrow crib, they
looked at their cute little girl and
said, "We love you just the same."

Then they picked her up, gave her a big hug
and kiss, and...
OOPS!
The little girl farted 200
butterflies!

The narrow parents ran all around the house chasing the butterflies, catching them and setting them free out the narrow window.

The narrow parents worried every day about what would become of their little girl who was not like everyone else.

They whispered to each other so no one would ever hear them say, "Our little girl farts butterflies."

The narrow aunts and uncles came to visit the new little girl. The aunts smiled, picked her up, gave her a big hug and...

OOPS!

The little girl farted 300 butterflies!

"She did what?!!!"
they screamed.
The little girl kept farting butterflies!

The aunts and uncles were horrified. They had never met anyone so *different*. They ran around the house, catching the butterflies and setting them free out the narrow window.

"Goodbye! We will not come back to visit," they said.

The poor parents took the little girl to a narrow park to sit and think on a narrow bench.

Then, an old, narrow lady came up to them and asked, "Why do you look so sad when you have such a beautiful little girl?"

Before the narrow parents could say anything, the old narrow lady picked up the little girl, gave her a big hug and…

OOPS!

The little girl farted 400 butterflies!

"She did what?!!!"

The narrow dogs barked and the cats meowed. One narrow cat even climbed up the narrow tree to catch a butterfly, but the branch broke and, OUCH! The cat fell flat on his narrow behind!

The old, narrow lady picked up the narrow cat and said, "Don't bring your daughter here again. She does not fit into our narrow park."

As the little girl grew,
the butterflies grew bigger
and BIGGER.

Her poor narrow parents became
so tired of chasing butterflies
around their narrow house.

When it was time to go to
the narrow school,
the narrow mother whispered
in the little girl's ear,

"Please promise me that you will not
fart butterflies, or everyone will know
that you are different."

The little girl promised her narrow
mother that she would behave herself
and not fart one butterfly.

When the little girl sat at her
narrow desk, nobody in the
narrow classroom smiled.

They all looked so bored reading
their narrow books, while
the narrow teacher was busy
writing on the narrow blackboard.

When the little girl went out to play in the playground, she remembered her mother's whisper, "Please don't fart butterflies." And she didn't.

But then a little boy looked at the little girl and smiled. He picked a flower and gave it to her with a hug and said, "I love you."

The little girl blushed. And...OOPS!

The little girl farted the BIGGEST butterfly in the world!

"She did what?!!!"
the children screamed.

The narrow teacher and all the narrow children ran around the narrow playground, trying to catch the butterfly.

When the narrow teacher reached up to grab the big butterfly, she fell and landed headfirst into the narrow sandbox.

All the narrow children laughed at the narrow teacher. The more they laughed, the more butterflies the little girl farted, until the whole narrow playground was full of butterflies!

The narrow police came in their narrow police cars to help catch the butterflies.

Then the narrow firefighters came in their narrow fire engines to see what had happened.

"She did what?!!!"
they all screamed.

Suddenly the big butterfly swooped down, lifted the little girl and started to fly high in the sky.

Everyone watched as they flew up to the dark, narrow mountains, where their points were poking through the clouds.

The narrow mother and father, who were afraid for their little girl, went running after the butterfly, followed by the little girl's narrow aunts and uncles, doctors, nurses, cats and dogs, and even the old narrow lady from the park.

Then something very magical happened.

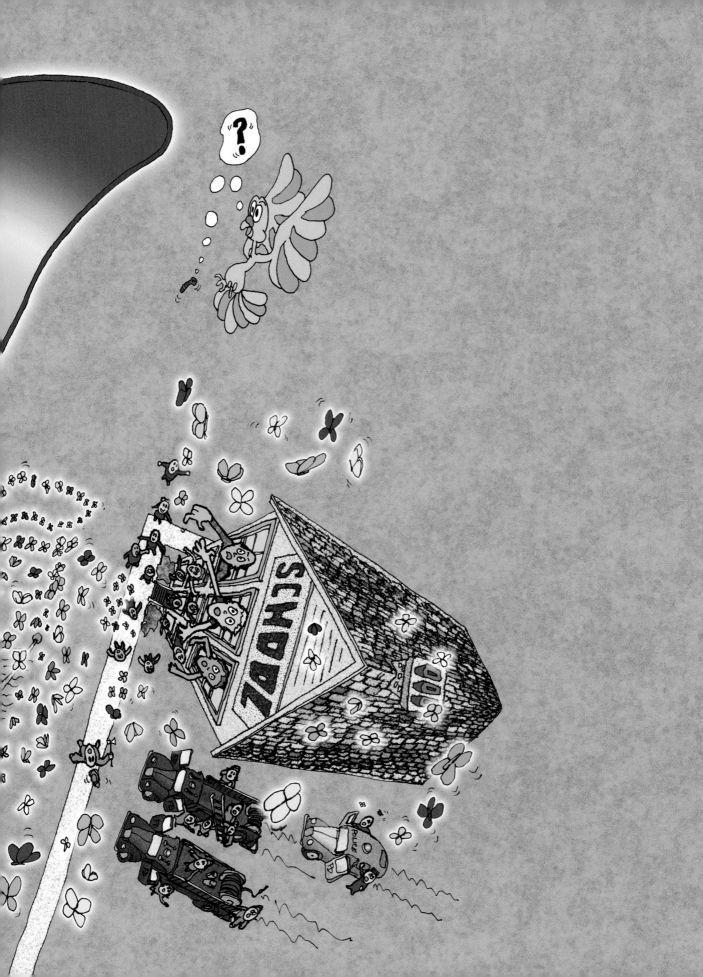

The little butterflies flew up and pushed
the dark mountains away so there
was lots of room to paint the sky with
their BRIGHT colours. Then the big
butterfly lifted the little girl high up in the
sky to write the word LOVE
against the sunset.

The whole town was surprised at what
this gifted little girl could do. Now
that the tall, narrow mountains were
gone, no one could believe how
much room they had and how wonderful
it felt to be nice and open.

Then the little girl blew a kiss to the little
boy. He was so happy that he
hugged the old narrow lady
from the park and...
OOPS!
They each farted
a butterfly!

When everyone saw what had happened,
they all started to hug each other.

The mother and father farted GOLD butterflies!
The old lady from the park farted a SILVER
butterfly!
The children in the school farted butterflies that
looked like RAINBOWS!
The firefighters farted RED butterflies!
The police officers farted DARK BLUE butterflies!
Even the little mouse farted. His butterflies were
POLKA DOT and looked like Swiss cheese!

Everyone was so happy to be loved that
they all became nice and wide.

So whenever you see someone
who is different from you, don't be afraid
to move out of your narrow house and
give them a BIG HUG!

Together with your heart,
you'll fart enough butterflies
to create the biggest,
the brightest and
the most beautiful sunset
in the sky coloured with...

LOVE!